Copyright © 1991 The Walt Disney Company

ISBN 0-88665-126-3

Printed in Hong Kong

2 3 4 5 6 7 8 9 10

Disney's
Beauty and the Beast

Twin Books

B. Mitchell

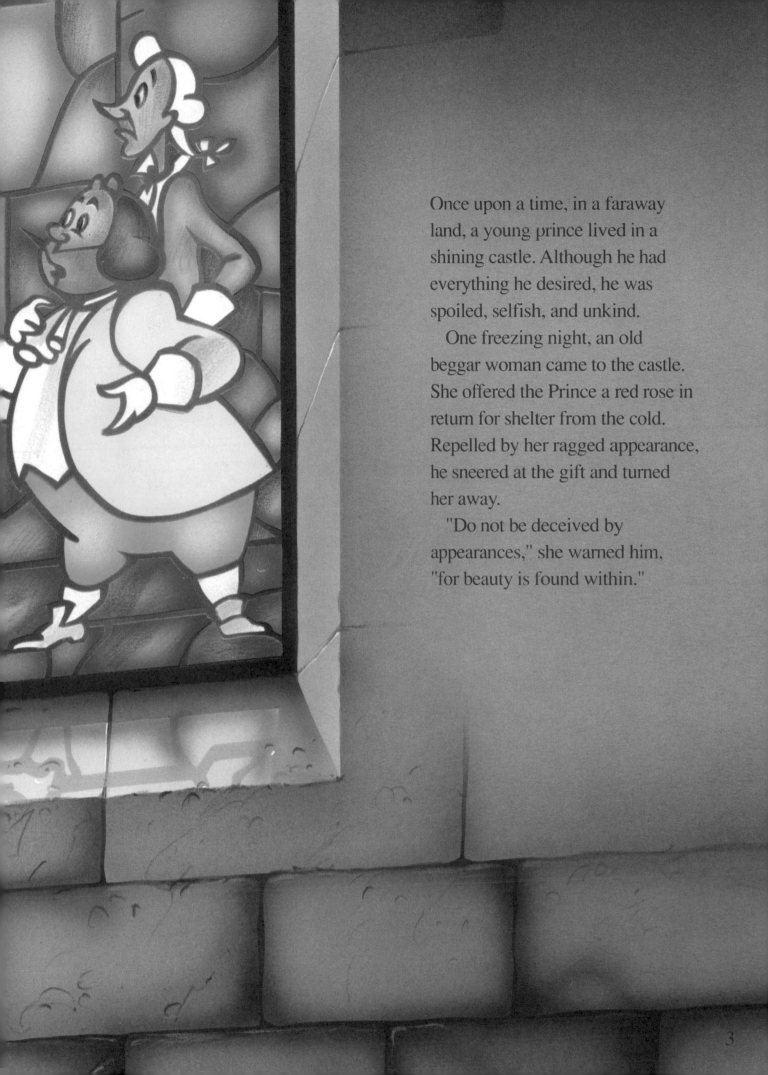

Once upon a time, in a faraway land, a young prince lived in a shining castle. Although he had everything he desired, he was spoiled, selfish, and unkind.

One freezing night, an old beggar woman came to the castle. She offered the Prince a red rose in return for shelter from the cold. Repelled by her ragged appearance, he sneered at the gift and turned her away.

"Do not be deceived by appearances," she warned him, "for beauty is found within."

3

The old woman was really an enchantress, who saw that the Prince had no love in his heart. As punishment, she transformed him into a hideous horned beast and placed a spell on everyone in the castle. Then she gave him an enchanted Mirror as his only window on the outside world. The Enchantress left behind the Rose she had offered him, which would bloom until his twenty-first year. For the spell to be broken, he must learn to love another and earn that person's love in return before the last petal fell. If not, he would remain a beast forever.

Not far from the castle was a charming little French village. There lived a beautiful girl named Belle, who loved to read about far-off places, daring sword fights, magic spells, and princes in disguise. She always had her nose in a book, and the villagers laughed at her, even though they liked her. Belle was so different from them.

One bright fall morning, Belle crossed the town square. She was too busy with her book to notice handsome, conceited Gaston, whom all the other village girls admired. But Gaston had noticed Belle. "Now *that's* the girl I'm going to marry," he vowed. "She's the only one who's worthy of me."

Just then, a loud explosion boomed from Belle's cottage. "Papa!" she cried, running for home.

In the smoke-filled cottage, Belle was relieved to find her father, Maurice, in one piece. "What happened, Papa?" she asked, gazing at the ruins of his newest invention.

"I'll never get this hunk of junk to work!" cried Maurice in frustration, giving his contraption a kick.

"Yes, you will, Papa!" said Belle.

The invention looked like an old armchair on wheels with a huge engine attached to it. A maze of pipes, whistlcs, bells, ropes, and pulleys erupted from the back. Inspired by Belle's confidence in him, Maurice seized a tool and went back to work.

That afternoon, as Maurice set off with the invention, Belle called after her father, "You'll win first prize at the fair!" Their patient horse, Philippe, carried Maurice and pulled the heavy cart behind them. A cold fog soon swallowed up the travelers.

Hours later, they were still on the road. Absent-minded Maurice pulled out his map and exclaimed, "This thing is printed upside down! We'll never get there. Come on, Philippe—let's take this shortcut through the woods."

Philippe whinnied nervously at the gathering darkness. Mist rose around them, and a cloud of bats took flight. Maurice looked back fearfully at the sound of prowling wolves, and Philippe reared up in alarm and lunged forward.

"Whoa, Philippe, whoa!" cried Maurice, as the terrified horse almost ran them over a cliff. Then Philippe heard a blood-chilling howl and threw off his rider!

Dazed by his fall, Maurice stared into the mist after the fleeing horse. Then the sound of approaching wolves roused him to action. He fled down a dark hillside, dodging gnarled branches and knobby roots, until he stumbled on a huge, ornate gate, rusty from disuse.

Desperately, he wrenched the gate open and fell through it, slamming it behind him just as the wolves attacked!

Breathless, Maurice crossed the neglected grounds of a forbidding castle and approached the door. When no one answered his knock, he stepped cautiously inside.

"Hello?" he called into the vast, echoing chamber.

"Not a word!" whispered a mantel clock to a golden candelabra.

"Oh, Cogsworth…have a heart," the candelabra replied. Then he called, "You are welcome here, Monsieur!"

Maurice was amazed to see a talking candelabra.

Maurice sank into a chair as Cogsworth looked around nervously for his master. Guests were *never* allowed at the castle. Then a tea cart arrived with Mrs. Potts, the teapot, and her son, Chip.

Suddenly, a huge, hulking figure stormed into the room and loomed over Maurice. "A stranger!" growled a savage voice. Then great clawed hands seized the terrified inventor and carried him to a dungeon!

At home in the village, Belle was awaiting her
father's return when there was a knock at the door. It
was the hunter Gaston, all dressed up. "Come in," said
Belle reluctantly. She didn't know that a crowd had
gathered outside to watch Gaston propose to her, then
marry her on the spot! Gaston demanded, "Say you'll
marry me!"

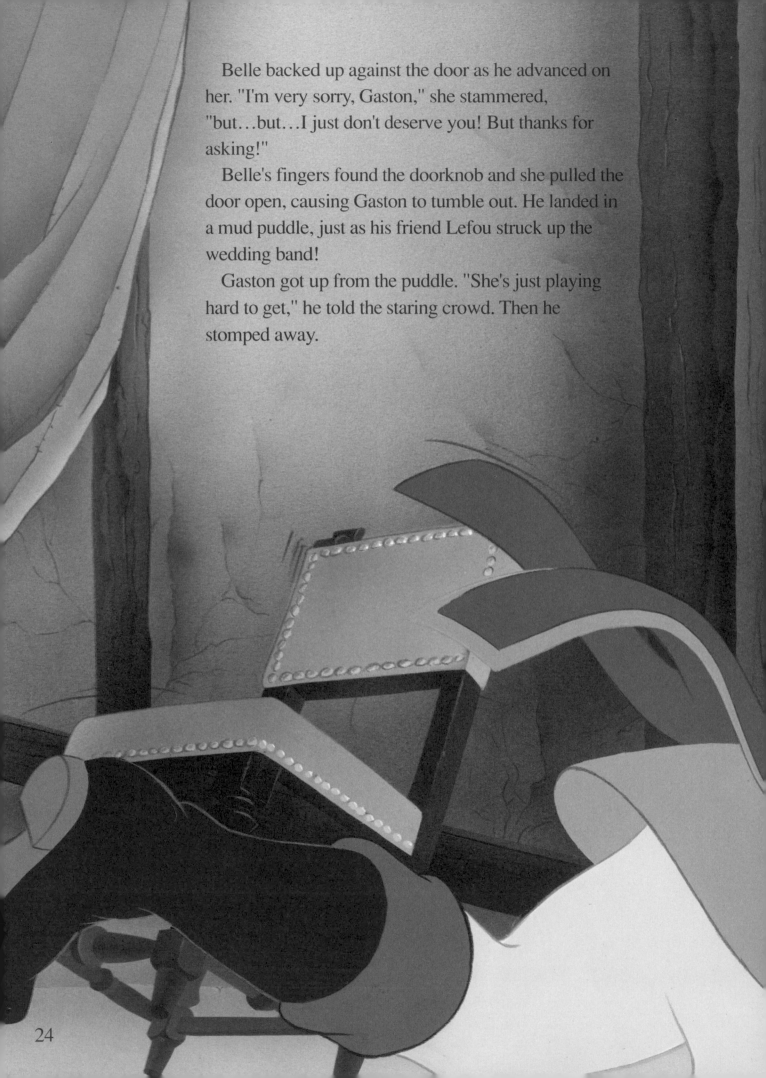

Belle backed up against the door as he advanced on her. "I'm very sorry, Gaston," she stammered, "but...but...I just don't deserve you! But thanks for asking!"

Belle's fingers found the doorknob and she pulled the door open, causing Gaston to tumble out. He landed in a mud puddle, just as his friend Lefou struck up the wedding band!

Gaston got up from the puddle. "She's just playing hard to get," he told the staring crowd. Then he stomped away.

After the crowd had gone home, Belle went into the
yard to feed the chickens. Hearing a familiar whinny,
she turned to welcome her father—and saw that
Philippe had returned alone!

"Philippe!" she cried. "Where's Papa?" The big horse snorted and whinnied anxiously.

"What happened?" asked the terrified Belle. "Oh, you must take me to him!"

Belle gathered her skirt and leaped astride the tired horse, who turned bravely and thundered back toward the dark forest.

Horse and rider plunged into the gloomy trees, but Philippe slowed down as they approached the crossroads. "Which way, Philippe?" asked Belle.

Reluctantly, Philippe headed downhill, into the mist-shrouded woods where he had left Maurice. Soon they arrived at the gates of the forbidding castle. "What is this place?" asked Belle in wonder.

30

Timidly, Belle entered the silent castle. "Papa?" she called. "Are you here? It's Belle." Cogsworth, Lumiere, and Mrs. Potts, astonished, followed her silently through the halls.

"Don't you see?" Lumiere whispered to Cogsworth and Mrs. Potts, "She's the one we've been waiting for–the one who will break the spell!"

At last, Belle found Maurice in the remote dungeon. "Oh, Papa," she exclaimed. "Your hands are freezing! We have to get you out of there."

Suddenly, Belle sensed danger and whirled around to see a massive shape in the shadows. "I'm the master of this castle," the Beast growled.

"Please!" she exclaimed. "Let my father out of here. He's sick."

"He shouldn't have trespassed here," replied the Beast.

"Then take me instead!" Belle demanded. The Beast stepped out of the shadows, and when she saw him clearly—she gasped in horror.

"You must promise to stay here forever," said the Beast.

"You have my word," Belle replied steadily, despite her fear.

"Belle, no!" cried Maurice. "You don't know what you're doing!" But the Beast dragged him from the cell and took him to the courtyard.

"Take him to the village," the Beast said to a palanquin, which trotted away with Maurice inside. Belle watched from the window, sobbing because she hadn't been able to say good-bye to her father.

The Beast returned to the tower to find Belle crying. "I'll show you to your room," he said gruffly, not knowing what else to do. As Belle followed him, he added, "You can go anywhere you like…except the West Wing. That's forbidden."

The Beast opened the door to a comfortable bedroom and said awkwardly, "You'll…uh…join me for dinner." Belle was left alone with the Wardrobe—who was thrilled to have a beautiful girl to dress.

"Well, now," said the Wardrobe cheerfully, "what shall we dress you in for dinner?" She flung open her doors.

"That's very kind of you," said Belle, gazing at herself in the Wardrobe's mirrored door. "But I'm not going to dinner."

"Oh, but you must!" cried the Wardrobe anxiously, just as Cogsworth appeared.

"Ahem! Dinner is served!" he announced importantly.

Downstairs, the Beast drummed angrily on the table, as his servants advised him to be patient with their visitor. "Master" said Lumiere, "have you thought that perhaps this girl could be the one to break the spell? You fall in love with her…She falls in love with you and—poof! The spell is broken. We'll be human again by midnight!"

"It's not that easy, Lumiere," said Mrs. Potts. "These things take time."

"It's no use," said the Beast. "But if she doesn't eat with me, then she doesn't eat at all!"

41

Back in the village, at the tavern, Gaston was brooding about Belle when Maurice burst into the room, muddy and wild-eyed. "Help!" he cried. "He's got Belle locked in a dungeon. We must go!"

"Slow down, Maurice," demanded Gaston. "Who's got Belle locked in a dungeon?"

"A beast!" cried Maurice. "A horrible, monstrous beast!"

The others burst out laughing, convinced that the old inventor was crazy. As two of Gaston's cronies were about to hustle Maurice to the door, Gaston narrowed his eyes in thought. Pulling Lefou aside, he said, "I have a plan…"

Later that night, Belle got very hungry. She found her way to the kitchen and heard the Stove complaining to Mrs. Potts: "I work and slave all day long, and for what? A culinary masterpiece gone to waste!"

Belle stared curiously at the Stove, which fell silent when it saw her.

"I *am* a little hungry," Belle confided to Mrs. Potts.

"You are?" cried Mrs. Potts excitedly. "Stoke the fire!" she called to Cogsworth and Lumiere. "Break out the silver! Wake the china!"

"Remember what the master said about feeding her," warned Cogsworth. But Mrs. Potts paid no attention to him.

"Right this way, Mademoiselle," said Lumiere,
leading Belle into the dining room. "Be our guest!"
With that, the bottles popped their corks, and the dishes
began to sing and dance with gusto as Lumiere
conducted! The Feather Dusters formed a lively
chorus line that swept up the sputtering Cogsworth.

It was a wonderful cabaret show, staged for the castle's first guest in ten years. Mrs. Potts bubbled with delight. The serving pieces brought in one delicious course after another.

When the banquet was over, Belle stood up and cheered. "Bravo! That was wonderful!" she exclaimed, clapping. "Now I'd like to look around, if that's all right."

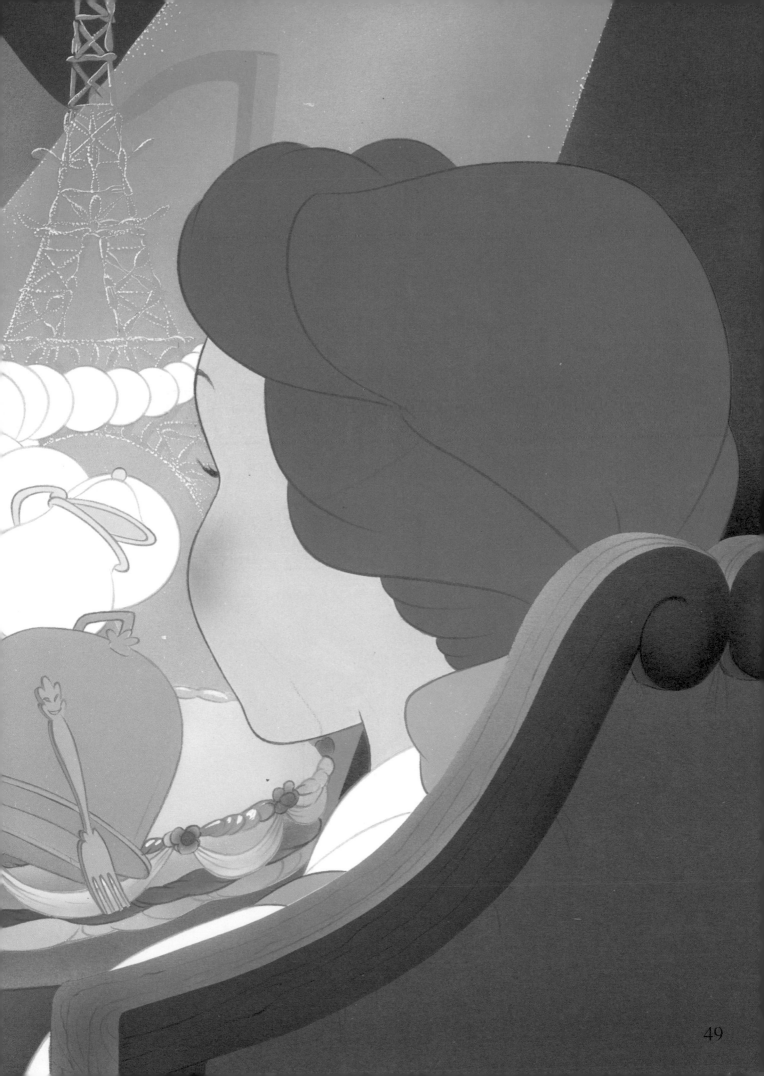

Belle had been warned not to go into the West Wing. But when the others weren't looking, she sped upstairs and entered the Beast's lair.

The dirty room was strewn with broken furniture, cracked mirrors, ripped clothes, and gnawed bones. The only beautiful, living thing was the enchanted Rose, glowing inside a bell jar. When Belle reached out to touch the Rose, the Beast leaped into the room!

"Why did you come here!" he roared. *"Get out!"*

Terrified, Belle turned and fled down the stairs. She
hurried outside and raced to the stable for Philippe.
They escaped from the castle into the freezing night.

Suddenly, Philippe snorted in alarm, and Belle saw cruel yellow eyes blazing in the dark. The wolves! Philippe broke into a frenzied gallop. Branches tore at them as they raced through the forest, with the wolves following close behind. Philippe reared in terror as a wolf snapped at his heels. Belle was thrown off, and Philippe's reins caught in a tree branch.

Belle seized a sharp branch to defend Philippe. As
the wolves closed in on Belle, a huge paw
snatched one wolf away–the Beast! He grappled with
the snarling wolves, flinging them to either side. The
forest echoed with the roar of combat.

The wolves were no match for
the Beast's fury. One of them bit
his arm before he sent it flying with
a sweep of his great paw. The wolf
slammed against a tree and lay still.
Then the rest of the pack slunk
away. The Beast staggered and fell
to the ground.

Belle knew that she could escape,
but when she saw that the Beast
was badly wounded, she stayed.

Supporting the Beast between them, Belle and Philippe went back to the castle. When Belle tried to put a compress on the Beast's arm, he roared, *"That hurts!"*

"If you'd hold still," said Belle, "it wouldn't hurt as much!"

"If you hadn't run away," sulked the Beast, "this wouldn't have happened." But he let her tie her scarf around his arm as a bandage.

"By the way," said Belle, "thank you for saving my life."

After that incident, the whole household was delighted to see a friendship growing between Belle and their master. First he showed her all the books in the huge library and said, "They're yours." The next day, Belle and the Beast had dinner together. Awkwardly, the Beast sat in a small chair and tried to eat with a spoon.

Later, Belle read the story of
King Arthur and Queen Guinevere
to the Beast. The tale was so
romantic that Lumiere cried. Even
Cogsworth wiped away a tear
before he sent everyone back
to work.

Soon afterward, the Beast shyly led Belle to the ballroom, where they danced to a beautiful love song. Then they went onto the terrace.

The Beast asked, "Belle, are you happy here…with me?"

"If only I could see my father again, just for a moment," Belle answered.

"There is a way," said the Beast, and he brought out the enchanted Mirror. When they looked into it, they were shocked to see Maurice lost in the forest, shaking with cold as he searched for Belle.

"Papa!" cried Belle. "Oh, no, he's sick and alone!"

"Then you must go to him," said the Beast. Handing her the Mirror, he said "Take it with you, so you'll have a way to look back…and remember me."

"Thank you for understanding how much he needs me," said Belle, touching the Beast's paw. Then she ran to the courtyard and rode away, as the Beast watched from his balcony.

When the Beast went inside, he said sadly to Cogsworth, "I let her go."

"You *what*?" cried Cogsworth. "How could you?"

"I had to."

"Why?" asked Cogsworth, near tears.

"Because I love her," sighed the Beast.

With the Mirror's help, Belle
found Maurice and brought him
home. He was delirious with fever
and dangerously sick.

When Maurice began to recover,
he could scarcely believe that the
Beast had let Belle go. "That
horrible beast?" he asked her in
amazement.

"But he's different now, Papa,"
said Belle quietly. "He's changed
somehow."

Just then, there was a knock on
the door.

Belle opened the door to see a strange man standing in front of the villagers and a van marked *Insane Asylum.* Monsieur D'Arque, director of the asylum, said, "I've come to collect your father."

"My father's not crazy!" said Belle angrily.

"He was raving about a huge beast!" said Lefou. He knew that Gaston planned to have Maurice locked up unless Belle agreed to marry him.

Belle ran into the cottage and returned with the Mirror. "Show me the Beast!" she demanded.

When the villagers saw the Beast in the Mirror, they screamed. Monsieur D'Arque sped away in his van, and Gaston seized the Mirror from Belle. Furious that his plan had failed, he told the villagers, "The Beast will make off with your children! He'll come after them in the night! I say we kill the Beast!" The mob cheered.

"I won't let you do this!" cried Belle. But Gaston locked her and Maurice in the cellar as the villagers gathered weapons and torches.

Guided by the Mirror, Gaston led the mob through the forest. On the way, they chopped down a tree to use as a battering ram. Cogsworth, Lumiere, and Mrs. Potts saw them from the window.

"*Sacre bleu!*" cried Lumiere. "Invaders!"

"Warn the master!" cried Cogsworth. "We'll be ready for them. Who's with me?" The others had already scattered to alert the household and prepare a defense.

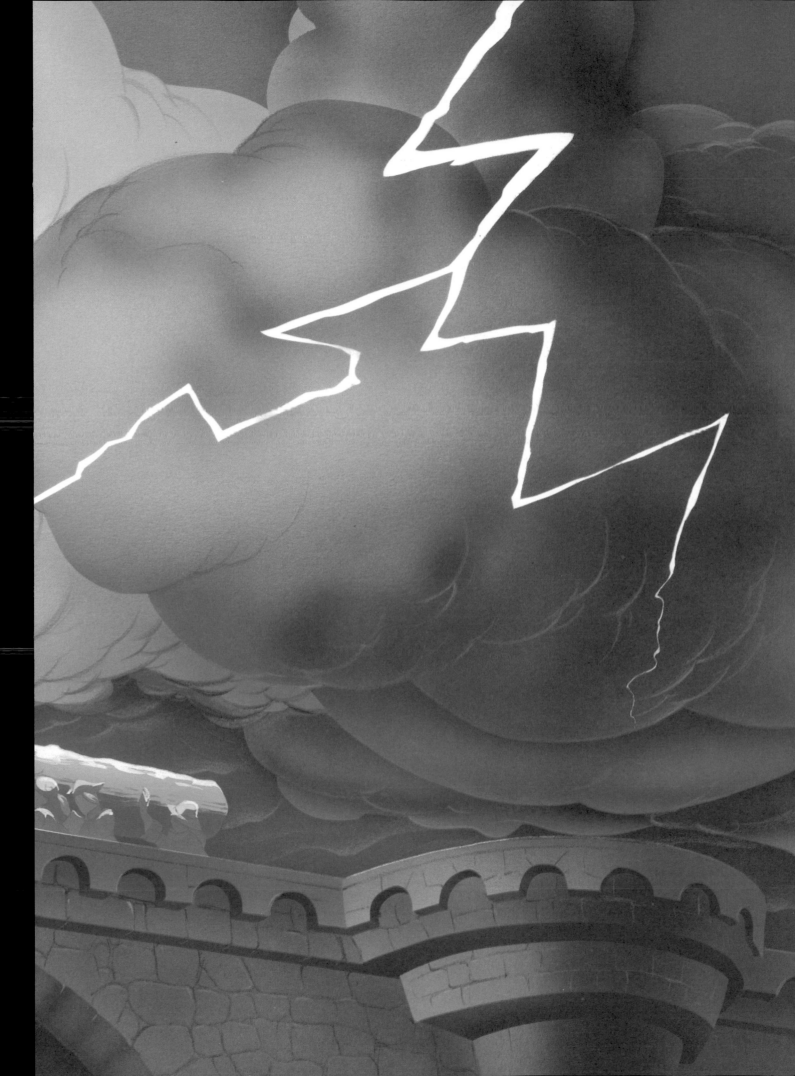

The battering ram crashed through the door, and the villagers entered the castle. At first, all was quiet. Then they were confronted by a host of angry Objects: pitchers and ladles, pots and pails prepared to do battle.

Upstairs, the Beast sat forlornly in Belle's room. "Leave me in peace," he said to Mrs. Potts when she came to warn him. A thunderbolt exploded in the sky as the villagers clashed with the defenders, but nothing could rouse the Beast to action.

As the fighting raged below, Gaston stalked the halls in search of the Beast. At last, the hunter found him in his lair. As the Beast faced Gaston, neither knew that Belle and Maurice were galloping toward the castle. Chip had stowed away in Belle's saddlebag before she returned to the village. When she and Maurice were locked up, he had used Maurice's invention to break down the door!

When Belle arrived, she saw that Gaston had forced the Beast onto the balcony. She watched in horror as he clubbed the unresisting Beast, driving him toward the edge of the steep roof.

"No!" cried Belle. She rode Philippe into the castle and up the stairs.

At the sound of Belle's voice, the Beast was roused to fight off his attacker. As
Belle reached his lair, he grabbed Gaston and gripped him tightly by the throat.
"Let me go!" pleaded Gaston. "I'll do anything!"

The Beast struggled with himself, but he had become too human to kill.
Growling, he pushed Gaston away and turned to Belle.

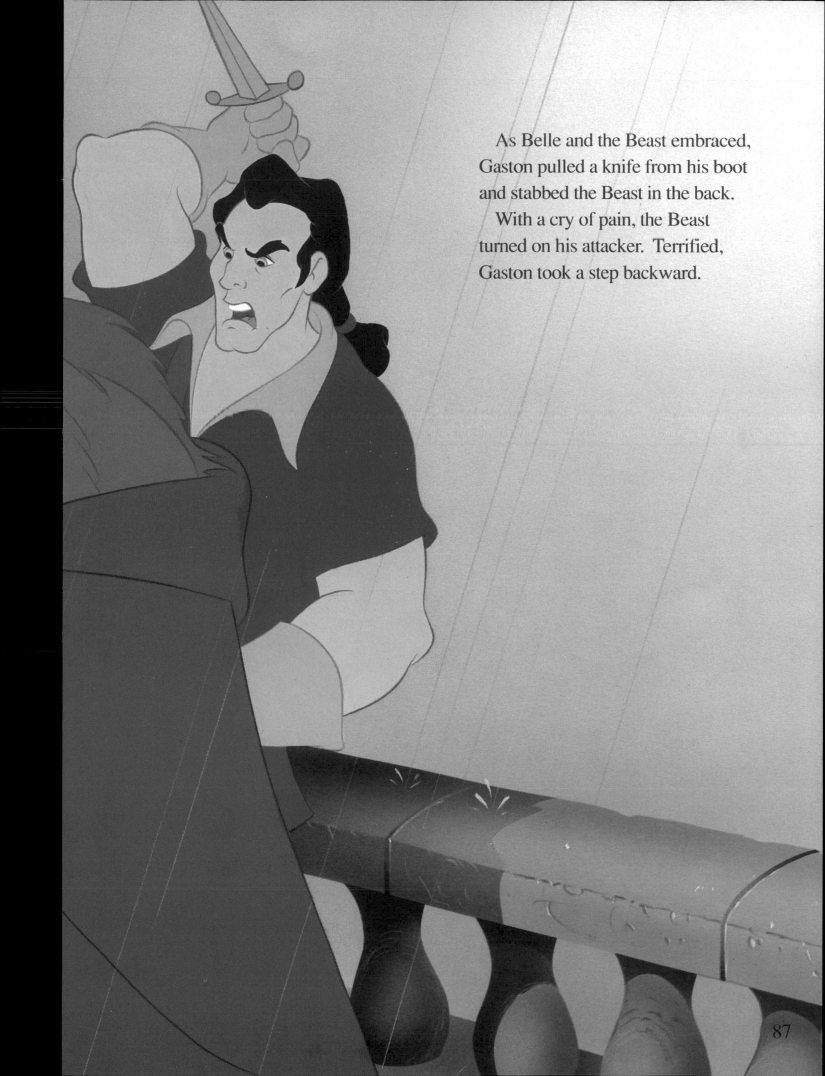

As Belle and the Beast embraced, Gaston pulled a knife from his boot and stabbed the Beast in the back.

With a cry of pain, the Beast turned on his attacker. Terrified, Gaston took a step backward.

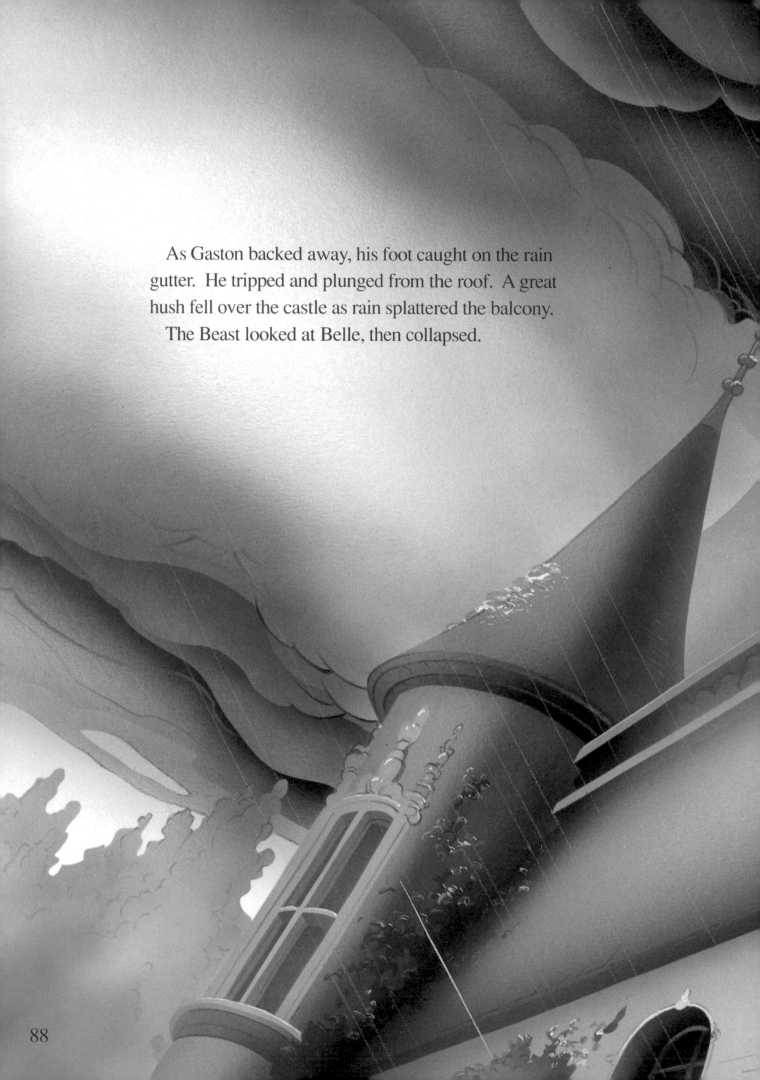

As Gaston backed away, his foot caught on the rain
gutter. He tripped and plunged from the roof. A great
hush fell over the castle as rain splattered the balcony.
The Beast looked at Belle, then collapsed.

Belle ran to the Beast's side and embraced him. "You came back," he said weakly, trying to smile. "At least...I got to see you one last time."

Struggling against tears, Belle cried, "Don't talk like that! You'll be all right." In the Beast's lair, the Rose's last petal was about to fall.

"Maybe it's better...this way," said the Beast.

"No!" cried Belle, overcome by tears. She leaned down to kiss him and said, "I love you."

As Belle wept, the last petal fell.
Suddenly, the rain began to
shimmer and sparkle. Belle
looked up and saw the air glittering
with magic.

The Beast's eyes blinked open.
His paws had been transformed into
human hands! He touched his face
and found that it was smooth. The
spell was broken! The wilted Rose
had burst into full bloom.

"Belle…it's me," said the Prince.

As Cogsworth, Lumiere, and Mrs. Potts looked on joyfully, the magic swirled around them, too. Cogsworth turned into a short, round, fussy major-domo with a moustache. Lumiere grew taller and taller, until a suave and dashing maitre d'hotel stood in his place. Mrs. Potts was transformed into the plump, smiling cook she had been before the spell. And Belle gazed happily at the handsome Prince, whom her love had restored to human form.

One by one, the members of the Prince's household became human again. They hugged each other with tears of joy, as the magic carried Belle and the Prince into the ballroom. There they began to dance.

Afterward, they stood on the balcony as the sun broke through the mist that had shrouded the castle for so long. The sun shone on the beautiful Belle and her handsome prince, whose love had finally broken the spell.